To Nan, love always

Bloomsbury Publishing, London, Oxford, New York, New Delhi and Sydney

First published in Great Britain in 2016 by Bloomsbury Publishing Plc
50 Bedford Square, London WC1B 3DP

This paperback edition first published in 2017

www.bloomsbury.com

BLOOMSBURY is a registered trademark of Bloomsbury Publishing Plc

Text and illustrations copyright © Tom McLaughlin 2016

The moral rights of the author/illustrator have been asserted

A CIP catalogue record of this book is available from the British Library

ISBN 978 1 4088 7015 0 (HB)
ISBN 978 1 4088 7016 7 (PB)
ISBN 978 1 4088 7014 3 (eBook)

All papers used by Bloomsbury Publishing are natural, recyclable products made
from wood grown in well managed forests. The manufacturing processes
conform to the environmental regulations of the country of origin

Printed in China by Leo Paper Products, Heshan, Guangdong

1 3 5 7 9 10 8 6 4 2

UP, UP and AWAY

Tom McLaughlin

BLOOMSBURY
LONDON OXFORD NEW YORK NEW DELHI SYDNEY

Orson was the kind of boy
who loved to make things.

And today he was going to make
something extraordinary.

BANG!

It would be his
greatest challenge yet!

A PLANET!

Orson, being an organised fellow,
first gathered together everything
he was going to need:

- a cup full of rocks

- a splosh of water

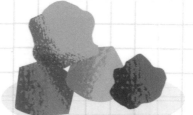

- a few chunks of metal . . .

and, since everyone knows that you need
lots of empty space for a planet,

nothingness

he gathered as much
nothingness as he could.

Now all he needed was a big bang
(which turned out to be much easier
to find than Orson had imagined).

There it was - a tiny planet
with rings around it.
Right there swirling
around his bedroom!

Orson loved his planet...

but his planet didn't look very happy.
It seemed to Orson that BUILDING a planet
was the easy bit. Looking after it –
well, that was a different matter altogether.

He tried to cheer it up,

but it still looked a bit
under the weather.

Orson needed some help, so he headed off to his
favourite place and found EVERY book on planets.

He read ALL through the night.

So, every day, Orson fed it.

He dusted its craters,

and tidied its oceans.

And it worked!
His planet seemed happy...

...and it began to grow.

Each morning it was a little bigger.
Soon it had moons!

And the more Orson cared for his planet,
the bigger and happier it became.

And that was when things started to get a little tricky.

His planet seemed to attract all sorts of things...

First it was just a few spoons
and the odd unicycle.

But soon EVERYTHING
wanted to join in!

You see, Orson hadn't realised,
the bigger planets get,
the more things get stuck to them.

That night, Orson went to bed
feeling as sad as his planet.

The next morning, Orson realised
he'd have to do something brave.

His planet didn't belong with him;
his planet belonged among the stars.

And although it was hard,
Orson knew that he was doing the right thing.

You see, sometimes you have to let go
of the things that you love the most.

But Orson wasn't sad for long.

Because Orson is a boy
who loves to make things,
and another idea had
just landed in his head.